CHAPTER 1

A First-Start Easy Reader

This easy reader contains only 43 different words,
repeated often to help the young reader develop
word recognition and interest in reading.

Basic word list for *You Look Funny!*

a	his	put
an	it	said
and	lion	so
are	long	stripes
bear	look	tail
coat	looked	the
day	made	them
ears	met	then
elephant	not	took
floppy	now	was
friend	off	way
funny	on	with
happy	one	you
have	panda	zebra
he		

You Look Funny!

Written by Joy Kim

Illustrated by Patti Boyd

Troll Associates

Library of Congress Cataloging in Publication Data

Kim, Joy.
  You look funny!

    Summary: Panda learns that ''Beauty is in the eye
of the beholder'' when he is criticized for his
appearance by all the animals except his own kind.
    [1. Pandas—Fiction] I. Boyd, Patti, ill.
II. Title.
PZ7.K5597Yo   1987   [E]   86-30839
ISBN 0-8167-0976-9 (lib. bdg.)
ISBN 0-8167-0977-7 (pbk.)

Panda was a bear.

He was a happy bear.

He was happy with
the way he looked.

Then, one day, he met an elephant.

The elephant said, "You look funny."

"You have funny ears."

Panda was not so happy.

So he made floppy ears.

He made floppy ears
and put them on.

Then, he met a lion.

The lion said, "You look funny."

"You have a funny tail."

Panda was not so happy.

So he made a long tail.

He made a long tail and put it on.

Then, he met a zebra.

The zebra said, "You look funny."

"You have a funny coat."

Panda was not so happy.

So he made a coat with stripes.

He made a coat with stripes
and put it on.

Then, he met a panda friend.

The panda friend said, "You look funny. You are a funny panda."

So Panda took off his floppy ears.

He took off his long tail.

He took off his coat with stripes.

He was so happy with the way
he looked.

And now Panda was a happy bear.